I'm a Big Brother Now

by Katura J. Hudson
illustrations by Sylvia L. Walker

Special book excerpts or customized printings can also be created to fit specific needs. For details, write or call the office of the Marimba Books special sales manager.

P.O. Box 5306 East Orange, New Jersey 07019 973.672.7701

MARIMBA BOOKS and the Marimba Books logo are trademarks of Marimba Books and Hudson Publishing Group LLC.

ISBN: 978-1-60349-014-6

Distributed by Just Us Books, Inc.   JustUsBooks.com

10 9 8 7 6 5 4 3 2 1

Printed in United States of America

MARIMBA
BOOKS

I'm a big brother now.

Mommy says I have one of the most important roles in the family.

My job as a big brother started
even before the baby was born.

When Mommy was pregnant,
I'd talk to her belly so the baby
would get to know my voice.

I helped Daddy
paint the baby's
room and put the
baby furniture
together.

I took care of Mommy, too.

I brought her favorite slippers, helped out around the house and made sure she drank a lot of water. The doctor said that was really important.

It was my job to make sure
Mommy's bag was by the door
so when the baby was ready,
we'd be ready, too.

And I knew how to dial 911
and call Daddy if the baby
came early.

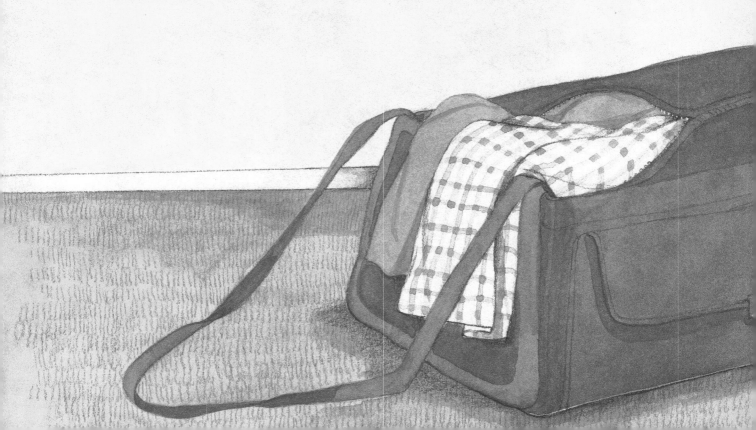

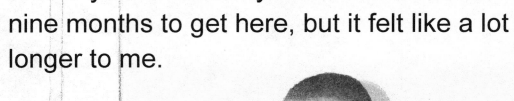

Mommy said the baby would take about nine months to get here, but it felt like a lot longer to me.

Finally, the day came. Mommy and Daddy went to the hospital. I stayed home with Grandma.

Late that night, Daddy called.
I was in bed, but I was too
excited to sleep.

So when Grandma came into the room and gave me the phone, I was ready to take Daddy's call.

"You're a big brother now,"
Daddy said. "How does it feel?"

I smiled.

"Good," I told him, and I meant it.

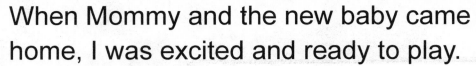

When Mommy and the new baby came home, I was excited and ready to play.

But Daddy said everyone needed rest.
So I kissed Mommy and helped her
put the baby down for a nap.

The baby slept a lot at first—
cried and ate a lot, too.

But soon, we were able
to do stuff together.

When I'd come home
from school, I'd tell
the baby all about
my day.

Or show off the latest moves I learned at basketball practice.

Sometimes I tripped, and that made the baby laugh.

And at night, Mommy, Daddy
and I read the baby my
favorite book.

I have a lot to look forward to, like camping and us playing my favorite games together.

But being a big brother
takes patience, and
a lot of work.

There are
lots of stinky
diapers,

and people
telling me
to **SHHHH**
because
the baby is
sleeping.

And sometimes that's hard, especially
when I want to do something fun

and Mommy or
Daddy says,
"Not now,
I have to
take care
of the baby."

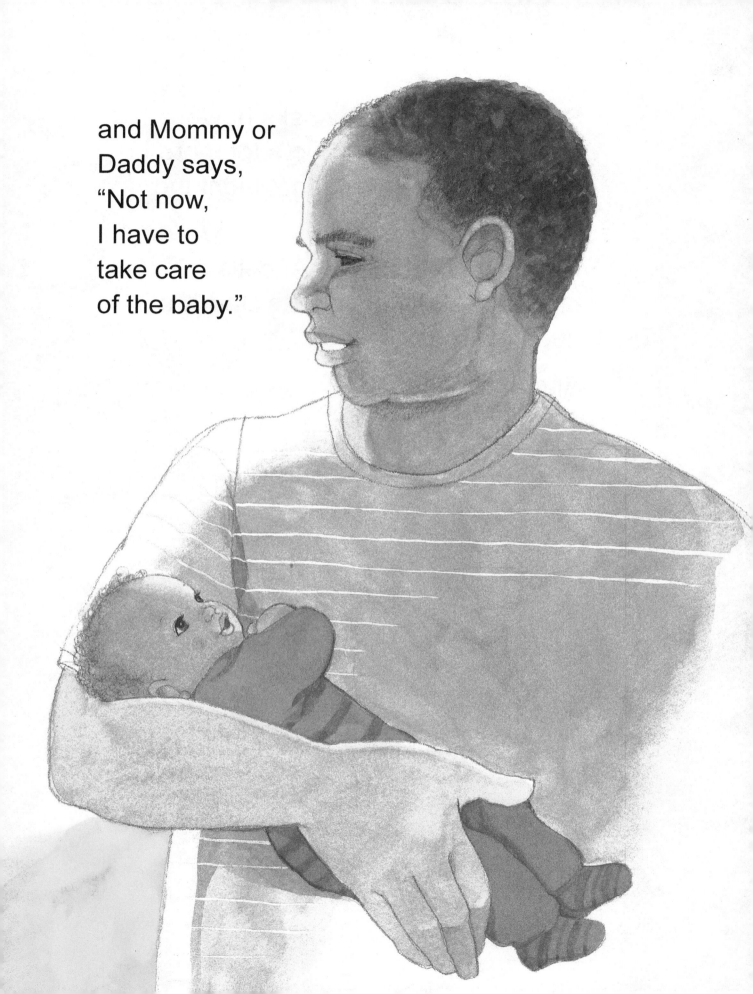

So now when Daddy asks how my new job is going, I have a lot more to think about than I did that night the baby was born.

I'm a big brother now. And it's a big job. But my answer to Daddy's question is still, "Good."

And I still mean it.

ABOUT THE CREATORS

Katura J. Hudson is a marketing professional, editor and original AFRO-BETS Kid. A native of New Jersey and graduate of Douglass College, Rutgers University, she has edited and led marketing campaigns for dozens of children's and young adult books. *I'm A Big Sister Now* is a companion to her first picture book, *I'm A Big Brother Now.*

Visit her at katurajhudson.com

Sylvia L. Walker is an illustrator and lifetime artist. She brings a natural affinity to the painting of multicultural images, especially children—expressing herself in a variety of media, including watercolor, pencil, ink, and acrylic on canvas. Sylvia earned her BFA at California Institute of the Arts and has more than 20 years of experience illustrating children's books and other work for clients including Hallmark Cards. Sylvia and her husband live in Culver City, California.

Visit her at sylviawalkerauthor.com

Dedication

For Kimaya and her big brother Christopher

For Anna and her big brothers Ben and Sam
–KJH

For big brother Scotty and his little sister Dana, the loves of my life
–SW

Cover design and display typography by Ty Nowicki

CPSIA information can be obtained
at www.ICGtesting.com
Printed in the USA
BVHW011006130921
616653BV00005B/51